Dragon Caller

Rise of the Archmage: Book One

By Michael D. Nadeau

Copyright © 2020 by Michael D. Nadeau

Acknowledgements

I would like to thank my wife and friends for inspiring me in my writing, as well as our games that have given this tale life.

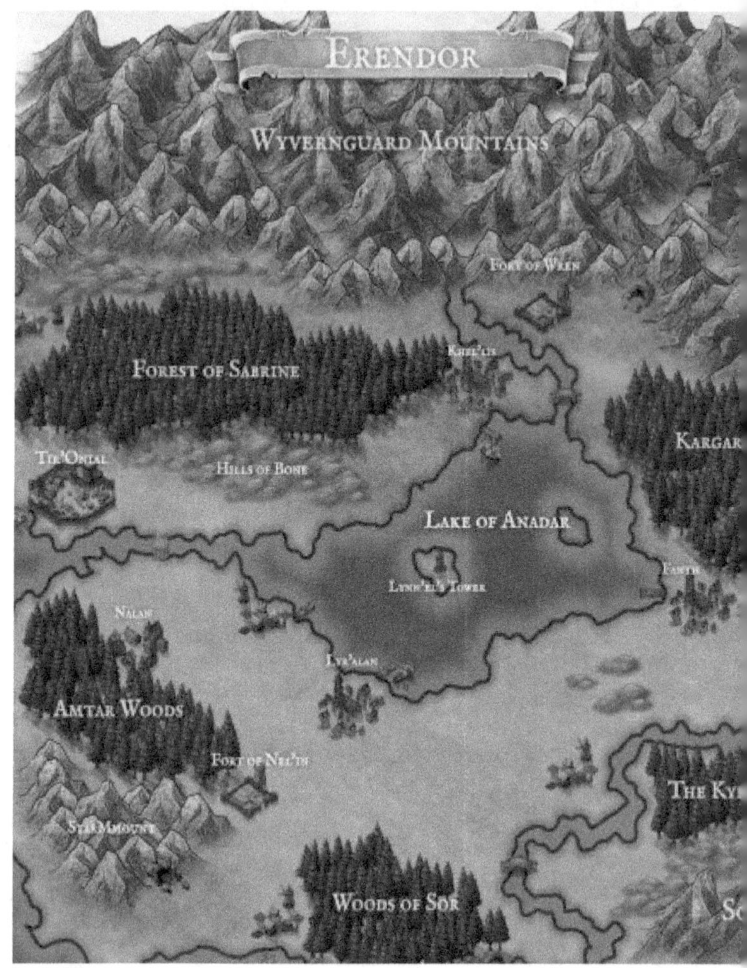
ERENDOR
WYVERNGUARD MOUNTAINS
FORT OF WREN
FOREST OF SABRINE
KHEL'LIS
KARGAR
TIR'ONTAL
HILLS OF BONE
LAKE OF ANADAR
LYNN'EL'S TOWER
FANTIR
NALAN
LYR'ALAN
AMTAR WOODS
FORT OF NEL'IS
THE KYR
SYR'MMOUNT
WOODS OF SOR
SO

Prologue
The Story

He sat in the chair opposite the small bed and took a deep breath, the book steady in his slender hands. "The story starts long and long ago, back when the land was covered in lush forests and..."

"Don't start the story like that, uncle, It's boring that way," the young child interrupted, sitting up in bed, frowning. "I want to hear the action parts first."

"Well, Nivia, that's not how stories are supposed to go. Yet I can see that we're not going to get anywhere unless I do...right?" He turned the pages of the ancient book, careful to keep the pages from wrinkling. Magic had made them resistant to the ravages of time, but they weren't immune to carelessness, even with those enchantments. Finally seeing where the events transpired to fit his niece's idea of action, he sat back once more and crossed his legs. He eyed her sternly, raising one eyebrow, and waited for what she was supposed to do.

"Oh...sorry uncle." Nivia lay back, pulling the covers back up to her face and shifted a couple of times. Once she was comfortable, she nodded to him and smiled. "Alright, I'm ready now."

"Very well little one," he said as he glanced out the window at Silen, goddess of the moon, hanging silently in the night sky. *So much has changed over the centuries, yet some things stay the same.* He returned his attention back to his niece, the title strictly honorary as she was so far removed that nothing else seemed to fit, and leaned forward in his chair to kiss her forehead. Sitting back, he placed the book in his lap and cleared his throat. The book felt light in his ancient hands, even after all these years. He knew this story intimately and his skin still had gooseflesh when he read it to one of his blood. It didn't matter that he knew the ending, it was the journey that thrilled him.

Chapter One
Returning to the world

The ground heaved and twisted as if the gods themselves had taken up their creation and shook it in anger. Pieces of rock broke away from his body and his fingers flexed for the first time in…well he wasn't sure. Another piece of rock broke away and he heaved stale, dusty air into unused lungs, coughing it right back out again in a fit that would've woken up an entire city, if there was one anywhere near him. *How long has it been,* he thought as he continued to free himself from his tomb, the walls still shaking as if it was an earthquake. Then, as quick as it had happened, it was over. He stood there looking at his surroundings and marveled at the sight.

He was in some sort of underground cavern, long stalactites reaching down to the floor as if yearning for freedom from their lofty prison. The rock was still encasing his feet and legs, yet his upper body was clear. He was stark naked, all of his clothes gone, yet his skin perfectly unmarred by whatever had happened to him. He searched around his encasing for his magic focus, praying that it too survived. He may have been blessed by the dark god, but that only helped him live through whatever had happened to him. He was still just an ordinary man, except that he couldn't be killed, and without his hand of power, he was trapped. Feeling around the cavity of stone, he finally found it, the shriveled elven hand still adorned with several precious stones set in its wrist. Some of the stones were shattered, an after effect of the power he had channeled through them in his last stand, yet the three that were left would be enough to break him free.

He took the quartz stone and placed it inside the severed hand, the fingers closing all on their own. *Good the magic still held*, he thought, feeling the power start to build in the hand as it waited for him. He pulled the forces around him, channeling them into the stone and focusing on the rock still encasing his feet. "Breken!" he shouted, using the elven word to command the earth to shatter the stone around him. He could only focus certain forces through certain stones, yet the dark god still smiled upon him it seemed. He still had his coral and jade stones as well, to focus water and mind spells, but he would have to gather more if he was going to enact his revenge upon the world by waking a dragon.

Ravin Dar stumbled free and worked the stiffness out of his legs, once again wondering how long he had been imprisoned in that stone tomb. He was naked, yet unharmed, his body fresh and whole. He had long black hair and deep black eyes that focused as he tried to orient himself after his ordeal. The last thing he remembered was making his last stand against the elven archmages atop the Starmount, a small mountain range in the southern part of Erendor. They had learned of his plan to raise a dragon and scour the world, catching him before he could even try. His mind was still a little fuzzy, yet he recalled one of the three archmages he was facing casting something with fire and stone...then his memory cleared; they had melted the very rock under him!

Ravin crouched down as the memory of the intense pain flooded back into him, the molten stone under him dragging him down into the bowels of the mountain. He clawed and fought to gain a hand hold, any purchase to stop his descent, so that he may cast something to pull him back out, yet the pain was too great. It had melted his clothes and burned his skin, his screams echoing in his own mind as it fully engulfed him, then he felt it start to harden, then...nothing; until now. He slowly stood, his resolve lending strength to his mission. He would get free and see what was left of the land, then resume his plans and bring this world to its knees.

Walking towards the wall of the cavern, Ravin felt air against his bare skin coming from a crack in the wall. He lifted up his hand of power and pulled power from the stones around him, focusing it into his will. "Cav!" The magic heeded his call and tunneled through the stone, creating a rough tunnel. He walked into the space as it comtinued, holding the hand of power in front of him like a beacon, directing the magic to continue on. Within minutes it broke into another tunnel and fresh air buffeted him, blowing dust into his eyes and lungs once more. Ravin coughed and sputtered, the magic falling out of his control, yet achieving the desired effect; he was that much closer to being free.

He stumbled on, seeing light in the distance and wondered what he would find. Soon, he walked into the bright sunshine of a new day, his long imprisonment over. The god of the sun, Sulan shone down upon him and when his vision cleared he took in the breathtaking view. The fields of high grass spreading out from him in all directions, he searched his memory for where he might start. *If I remember, there was a town due east of the Starmount.* Ravin stood straight and acutely realized his nakedness as the cool air washed over him. "Sorone guide me," he said, calling upon his dark god for the first time since being freed. When nothing happened, he shrugged and walked on towards his destiny.

LATER THAT NIGHT, RAVIN walked into a small village to the stares of its people. He ignored them, striding towards the main hall situated in the middle of the village. Torches burned, lighting his way, and people bustled to and fro, finishing their chores and duties for the day before the moon rose to high. The main hall was a building usually used for village announcements and meetings in his day, and no matter how long it had been, he was fairly certain they still used them for something. He smiled when the two guards walked towards him, hands on their weapons and confusion on their human faces. They carried torches as well and had deep blue cloaks with a silver clasp of a sword. *Weird,* he thought as he slowed at their approach, *I haven't seen an elf yet.*

"Hold traveler. How fare thee in your travels that you have come unclothed to our village?" one guard asked as the other one slowly kept circling so as to keep him contained.

"You two seem very competent for such a backwater village," Ravin said, still holding his severed elven hand in his hands. He kept it low, hopefully out of sight for now.

"We're part of the Riders of Erendor sir, and right now we need to know what befell you out there." His partner had drawn his weapon as quietly as he could, yet Ravin still heard the slight scrape of steel on the metal ring of the scabbard.

"Why nothing befell me out there." He turned then, eyeing the guard and his sword with a raised eyebrow and smirked. Turning back, Ravin bowed to the first guard and put on an act of obedience. "Good sir, might you have a cloak I could borrow?" He could see some of the women of the village gathering, obviously staring at his nakedness. *Good. Give them something to dream about tonight in their lonely, cold, beds.*

They offered him a cloak and he hid the hand of power within its folds as he covered himself. "Thank you. Now, might I speak to your lord?" he noticed that the guard behind him sheathed his sword as well. He was making progress.

"Our lord sits on the council in Tir'Onial, yet we will escort you to the village baron." The guard waved his hand for Ravin to walk with him and took his hand off of his weapon.

"Tir'Onial still stands? That is good news," he said as they walked. "Yet the council is unknown to me. Tell me, when did they abolish the elven king?" Ravin knew he had said the wrong thing as both guards stopped, hands right back to where they were.

"How do you not know of the council?" the second guard asked, his sword coming out once more.

Ravin quietly took the quartz stone out of the hand and tried to place the jade in, knowing the feel of the shape from long use.

He finally got it in and turned, whispering to the first guard. "Loktar." He saw the man's eyes slowly glaze over and visibly relaxed. It would be hard to see in the torchlight. "I came by ship from the south."

"Basker, leave thy weapon sheathed." The first guard let go of his and smiled. "You must be from the southern continent. Come let's go to the baron now."

"So when did they institute a council in this fair land?" he asked a couple of streets later, seeing that the second guard deferred to the one he could now control.

"After the sorcerer, Ravin, was thrown down in the Starmount in the battle of fire and stone. They reset the year then, and ever since they have used the council instead of a king." The first guard said, not even looking back at Ravin.

It was strange hearing his name used like that in history and knew deep down that many years must've passed indeed, yet he needed to know how many so he could gauge who his allies and enemies would be. "And the current year is?"

"Hanel, this is too strange indeed," the second guard said, slowing his pace. "No ships have come from the south in many years and to not even know the year?"

Hanel ignored him and walked on. "It is currently the nine hundredth and fifteenth year of A.R."

"A.R.?"

"After the Fall of Ravin of course." Hanel said as Basker drew his weapon once more, this time pointed at Hanel.

"He has you enthralled Hanel, though I know not how." Basker stepped sideways away from Ravin and held his sword up on guard. "You there, Goodman, get the baron's guards, I need assistance," he called to a man walking by with a fishing cage.

Ravin shook his head sadly. It was going so well too. "Hanel, your friend Basker is going to strike down an unarmed man. Kill him." Ravin saw the command widen Hanel's eyes as the man fought the power of the mind magic, so he held the hand under his cloak once more and channeled more power through it. "Loktar!"

"Basker, you stand in defiance of the laws of the land and must suffer the penalty of treason," Hanel said, drawing his weapon and advancing on his friend.

Ravin watched, backing away and joining the gathering folk as the guards fought. One with fierce determination, the other, confused desperation. Swords clashed and steel rang out as they fought in the dim light, their own torches forgotten on the dirt path beneath their stomping feet. They were evenly matched and the fight dragged on, even as the baron's guards came jogging down the lane in their studded armor. Ravin went to meet the head of the guard, as the others called to the Riders of Erendor to cease.

"What is the meaning of this?" the head guard asked, eyeing Ravin and the cloak he wore. "What are they doing?"

Ravin whispered the elven word for controlling the will of others once more and focused the magic at the head guard, weaving a plausible story of sickness and madness. He stepped back as the head guard raised his crossbow, motioning for his fellows to do the same.

Basker finally deflected his partner's blade out wide and rammed his own sword through the opening near the arm, the steel finding the lungs quickly. He leaned on his sword, his lungs heaving and looked up as the head guard pointed the ranged weapon right at him. "No...wait!"

"Fire!"

Five bolts thudded into Basker's chest and neck, dropping him quickly. He lay there, hand on his neck trying frantically to stop the blood from escaping. He mewed softly and in seconds was gone, his lifeless eyes staring into the night sky.

"Thank you captain, now can you escort me to the baron? I have dire news for him." Ravin smiled at the glazed look in the captains' eyes, yet his mind was in a tumble. It had been over nine hundred years! Surely everyone he knew and loved was gone, yet his enemies would be as well. Elves lived for a long time, but the archmages were old even then. *A fresh start it is then, with no one to know what is coming...delightful.*

Chapter Two
Path of destiny

The elf danced away from the woman's embrace, his grace apparent to any who could see him move. The woman was undeterred, however, and sauntered after him with a lust in her blue eyes that was rarely seen in her these days.

"You tease me, fair wizard. Come to me and show me your talents." The woman was in her fortieth summer, yet still attractive. She had long brown hair tied in a bun and wore nothing but a violet scarf around her neck.

"Countess Veriga, your beauty alone has me swooning, and yet I hesitate," The elf said, also dressed in nothing but a white silk scarf tied around his slender waist and an anklet fitted with eight tiny stones. He spun once more, his white hair flowing around him like silk in the summer winds.

"Why do you hesitate to pleasure me so?"

"Because I fear I will lose myself inside of you and never return," the elf replied, flashing his silver eyes at her as he danced closer. He was just out of her reach now and he dragged his slender fingers across her back as he twirled by her, her shiver easy to see to his trained eyes. He had her right where he wanted her and he had to admit, he would enjoy this as well.

"Salen, please..." she begged, turning towards him once more. "Come here and let me show you what the years have taught me about pleasing a man."

Salen smiled and did indeed glide towards her, whispering upon the wind and focusing the magic through the charms around his anklet. "Fra," he said, using the elven word for wind and channeling his power into the peridot stone. A gust of wind blew off her scarf revealing her breasts and leaving her vulnerable to his hands at last. Not that she was that vulnerable...she outweighed him by three stones at least.

Lady Veriga Halas wrapped her arms around his slender body as Salen embraced her fully, his kisses falling upon her slender neck. "Oh, you are indeed as worked up as I am, aren't you, wizard?"

"In truth lady, I do indeed want this as much, if not more than you can imagine." He kissed her deeply, angling her towards her wrought iron bed as they twirled. The canopy was draped in white silk and gold trim and they bounced as they landed upon the silk sheets. They lay there for hours, his skill and her lust dragging it on well into the early morning. When he fell back upon the bed once more, he saw that Lady Veriga was already snoring, deep exhaustion taking her quickly. It was a good thing Lord Halas wasn't due into the city for another day at least. *Honestly, I will never understand why these humans ignore their wives as they age...she was quite talented.*

Salen rose and dressed, donning his white silk doublet and black breeches. He walked to the door, throwing on his dark leather longcoat and snatching up the large emerald necklace he was there to procure for his master, and then danced out the door and down the hallway of the Halas Villa. No guards stopped him, after all they all saw him come in with the lady of the estate, and soon he was on his way back to the tower of his master, errand completed. The elven wizard stopped at the edge of the villa and looked out over the capitol city of Tir'Onial and smiled. It was a fine morning already.

Salen Valari was a wizard, and quite a talented one at that. A prodigy among his peers, he mastered the stones necessary to channel magic faster than anyone they had seen, already attaining seven of the eight stones in just under fifty years. He was apprenticed to the Archmage Lynn'el, one of the oldest elves in all of Erendor, and was well on his way to attaining the title of archmage himself. He just had to learn a little restraint, or so his master said.

Elven wizards of Erendor channel the forces of the world around them by focusing that power into precious stones matched to those forces. This is inherent to all elves, bound in blood by an ancient pact, and cannot be taught to anyone not of elven blood. However, a wizard can only channel so much power through these stones and if pushed too far, they will detonate, throwing the magic back onto the caster. This is why the elves take centuries to master the stones, attuning themselves to them and the power they represent. Salen, by that measure, was utterly remarkable and the target of every slur that the other wizards could come up with. He never minded, they were colorful at least and half of them were true.

He walked down the cobblestone streets of Tir'Onial as Sulan, god of the sun fought to rise and watched the folk get ready for their daily tasks. He was over one hundred and thirty years old and very attractive, yet seen as soft by the human workers that he passed. His master had always told him to dress more like a wizard, thus affording the respect he deserved, but he disdained that look, favoring his dusty longcoat and his slim sword over the robes and staff of the wizards. *I'll gain my own respect and reputation,* he thought as the men and women openly sneered at him, thinking him nobility. They weren't all wrong.

Salen was indeed noble, at one point. His parents were part of the council for years, with House Valari ranking very high in the city indeed. Sadly, they died at sea over ten years ago in a freak storm, leaving him alone and without other family to help maintain his claim. The other houses descended like vultures and soon he was without title and money. He patted the sword at his hip and smiled, knowing that his father would be proud that he carried it, despite losing the family title.

"About time you finished with that old bat," a voice called out from the side of the road.

Salen recognized the voice of his old friend immediately, yet didn't bother to look. He knew that the half-elf would be so well hidden that he wouldn't see him anyway. "Somrael, are you spying on me?" It was asked in fun, for Salen knew that if the half-elf wanted to spy on him, he would never have known about it without magic.

"No, I was just waiting to make sure that you weren't chased out of the house by the lord like that last time," the dark skinned half-elf said. He was dressed in black breeches and a grey shirt, his cloak a deep black with a large hood. His faded grey hair and beard were the only signs of his mixed heritage, as well as the Jet stone on his necklace dangling from its silver chain. Somrael Anar was also a wizard, though just a novice.

Half-elves, though they had elven blood in their veins, couldn't control the forces of the world as well as elves could. They were only able to master one, or two stones at most, with ease. If they attempted any more than that, they usually lost control of all of them and had to start over again. With a lifespan only a little longer than humans, they didn't really have the time for that, so most stopped at one stone. Somrael had chosen the jet, as it was tied to shadows.

"That was once and he never caught me," Salen said, laughing at the look on his friend's face as he came fully into the road. Most elves didn't like their half cousins, seeing them as half breeds and failures. Salen didn't care about that as long as the person showed himself to be a worthy friend. Somrael had done that, and more, over the years and the two had become fast friends.

"So did you get it?"

"Yes, I got it. Even had a bit of fun as well."

Salen, get to the tower as quickly as you can, something's happened...

The voice of his master echoed in his head as the magic of the jade stone faded. With jade, one could use the magic of the mind, either to speak to another's mind, or control them. He rubbed his temples as he considered how best to get there the quickest.

"I know that look, what happened?" Somrael looked around nervously as if he was expecting a flood of trouble any minute.

"It was Master Lynn'el. She says something's happened and to get to the tower." Salen turned around and headed for the harbor, intending to take a small ship up river to the lake of Anadar where his master's tower rested.

"I still think it's weird that you call her master instead of mistress," Somrael said, making conversation as they walked.

"It is one of her rules, and the strictest one at that."

"She's weird."

"She's ancient and powerful. If she wants me to call her Flabigast then that is what I'll call her," Salen said, dodging the morning rush of people. He had wanted to be long gone before the people started filling the streets of Tir'Onial, but one doesn't always get what he wants. They made their way to the docks and found at least three captains with their sail signs already posted.

A sail sign was a small plaque that the captain of a ship put out to let people know his craft was ready for hire, what the typical payment was, and what they specialized in if anything. If a sign was out, the ship would be expected to sail within minutes of the transaction and it helped people to find the right type of ship for the funds they had. Of course the price was always negotiable, but it helped to have a starting point sometimes.

Salen spotted a familiar face and walked right to the ship, bypassing others without a second glance. "Well, well, Captain Greyson, I see you're packed and ready to go this fine morning?"

Captain Thandyr Greyson was a brute of a man, an adventurer of many years who finally settled down and bought a small ship named the *Mist Runner*. He stood and kicked his sign over, ignoring the look on the wizard's face. "My sign isn't up. Go away wizard."

"I see he is still a man of many words, Salen," Somrael said laughing.

"Not helping, Som." Salen bent and picked up the sign, dusting it off and placing it back on the dock. "Look Thandyr, I need to get to Lynn'el's tower and you're the fastest ship up the river."

"The last time you hired my boat we almost died!"

"Oh come now, those pirates only wanted me. Besides, I kept the damage minimal didn't I?" Salen cringed inside as the man started shaking, his face turning red, yet he needed this ship right now. "Look, I'll double your price."

Thandyr stopped shaking and just stood there, his breathing slowing down. "Double?"

"Heh, that got his attention," Somrael said, counting out the silver cylinders.

Wizards didn't trade in coin like most people. Instead, they used cylinders of silver and gold, carved out of the raw material by using magic. Each cylinder was a one inch core of the material and was the same as two coins of the same material.

"You heard me. Forty silver cylinders to bring me up the river to the tower." Salen smiled at him and held out his hand to his friend. The bag was placed on his open palm and Salen brought it around in front of Thandyr.

The captain took it and held it aloft, as if weighing it in his mind. He sighed heavily and picked up his sign. "All right, let's get this trip underway and quickly," he said, shaking his head. "I'm going to regret this, but the money is good," he said to himself.

Salen and Somrael walked up the boarding plank to the *Mist Runner*, its wide deck and discolored mast seeming out of place with the rest of the ships docked there. The stares of most of the other captains only made them smile and in a matter of minutes, they were underway.

Salen stood at the bow and closed his eyes. *I'm coming Master,* he thought, worried for the first time in his apprenticeship. Lynn'el had never sounded so tense before and it was throwing him off.

Chapter Three
My own Life

She stomped down the marbled hallway and slammed the doors to her room open, storming in and throwing her sword on her bed. Shyi-Lhanna Nightstar was in one of her moods again, brought on by her mother, as always. Shyi huffed and threw off her practice armor, not caring that it landed on the floor or not. She was too angry to care about that right now.

"You get back here young lady!" The voice of Eliana Nightstar echoed down the hallway as she chased her daughter. "You will not be entering the tournament and that is final!"

Shyi's eyes widened at the sound of her mother. The esteemed lady of the Nightstar villa had never chased after her daughter when they argued before. Shyi turned and slammed the doors to her room closed, sliding a chair in front of them as she smiled wickedly. "Can't talk right now *mother*...I have to bathe regularly as is expected of a woman of my *stature*." She heard her mother speak the word for wind and backed up, suddenly worried. She had never seen her mother angry enough to use magic inside the villa, let alone the very room she was in. She knew the door wouldn't hold, yet the young elf stood defiant by the far wall. She wouldn't be cowed by a wizard, even if it was her mother.

The door crashed in, a wind howling through the opening and filling the room before dissipating. Eliana stood there, chest heaving as she stared at her daughter. "You are too young to be playing at these dangerous games, daughter."

"I'm almost ninety-five, mother," Shyi said, folding her arms across her chest. Her long white braids falling over her shoulders. "Just because I refuse to become a wizard like you—"

"And every woman of my line," her mother interrupted.

"—doesn't mean that I'm abandoning the family!" Shyi walked towards her mother, dropping her arms and hardening her jaw. "Mother, I have no desire to channel magic. I've trained with the sword since I was twenty, besting all my tutors and even giving father a run once or twice. That tournament is the pinnacle of skill in Tir'Onial and I can win it."

"Yes, but..." Eliana began, yet stopped when Shyi held up her hand to forestall her.

"Mother, enough. Why can't you accept me for who I am?"

"Because, Shyi-Lhanna, you are an elf and my daughter, both of which cry out for you to learn the magic that has ruled women of my family line for centuries."

"That's no reason to rule my life!" Shyi screamed, stepping right up to her mother's face. If she used what her father taught her about forcing someone to step back and reassess, then she may get through to her. She underestimated the woman completely. The slap came quick, quicker than Shyi would've thought and caught her full on the side of the face. Just the sound of it echoed in the now silent space they occupied and all that anyone could hear was their breathing.

"Shyi...I'm..."

Shyi stood swiftly, coming up from a crouch with a closed fist and extending her arm, catching her mother off guard. A hand caught her fist at the last moment, stalling her momentum and taking the brunt of the force behind the punch easily. Her father had come out of nowhere, his expression grave, as he stood between the two women like a wall.

"Enough! Both of you!" Haran Nightstar said, his whole body screaming authority.

"Haran, she..." Eliana tried, but her voice faltered under his stern gaze as he turned towards her, still holding his daughter's fist.

"Lorial, take me," he said, using his goddess's name in vain. "You struck our daughter over wanting a different path than you?" He turned his gaze back to Shyi and let go of her hand and continued. "And you! You would've hit your mother?" He walked further into the room, leaving them facing each other and their own shame and stood at the window, staring out at the sight of Sulan, hanging in the sky. "What happened to the sweet girl of twenty years ago?" he asked, leaving them both to wonder which one he was referring to.

Shyi was still seething though, and knew that she needed to cool off before she said anything further. "I'm going to find work until the tournament in two tendays," she said, gathering up her sword and a few things from her personal locker at the foot of the bed. "And no, I won't be home between then and the tournament."

"If you walk out that gate... do not come home." Eliana's voice was deep and final, surprising even her husband.

"Now Eli, let's not..." Haran never finished as his wife of four hundred years turned and walked out of the room, her back to the both of them.

"I'm still going, father," Shyi said, tears welling up in her bright violet eyes.

"You will always be welcome here, daughter," he said, embracing her in a tight hug. "She'll calm down once you're gone and come around eventually." He meant the words, she could tell, yet there was a note of hesitation in his voice.

"And if she doesn't?"

"Then *my* daughter will always be welcome in *my* house."

"Don't say that, you two love each other, father! She just hates me that's all."

"She doesn't hate you; she's just upset that her family legacy will die with her. Be safe out there and come home before the tourney so I can fit your horse. I know that you can take care of yourself," he said, drawing his own sword and handing it to her in reverence, "but take Mithsran and wield it with honor Shyi. I've heard the Riders of Erendor are looking for able warriors to patrol the land."

Shyi was taken aback. Her father's sword was his most cherished weapon, serving him for centuries. "I will honor you father and bring fame to house Nightstar," she said, as was customary in the exchange. She had learned some things after all her training. They embraced quickly and he left, his strong shoulders shaking as he exited her room. Shyi-Lhanna had never seen her father cry before.

SHYI RODE OUT OF TIR-Onial that evening, tears falling from her violet eyes. She wore her silver chased armor, denoting her family crest of House Nightstar, and carried the sword Mithsran at her side. She hadn't gone very far when the sound of another rider reached her ears. Wary of the timing, she pulled her horse around and faced the oncoming rider, hand on the hilt of her blade.

"Ho the rider!" the man called out, slowing as he approached. "I come as a traveler not an opponent," he started, his hands where she could see them. He was a large man, human, and easily almost seven feet tall if he was an inch. He seemed to weigh as much as twenty stones by his size, and his great sword on his back looked more like the side of a wagon than a weapon. Shyi kept her silence as he brought his horse closer, now within striking distance. "I'm traveling to the Fort of Nel'in to join the Riders of Erendor," he said, bowing slightly as he talked. "It's a four day ride, at best, and I could use the company if you're headed that way."

Lorial's fate, or Ta'ar's scheming, she thought, which god wanted him to be headed to the exact same place as I am this very day. Shyi let go of her sword though and put on her best snarl. *It matters not which god or goddess did; I can take care of myself if need be.* "Very well, good sir, but you can take point with that hunk of steel you think is a weapon."

"And your name, fair maiden?" he asked, his smile infectious.

"Though I am no fair maiden, my name is Shyi-Lhanna. What is yours, good warrior?"

"The name is Rikard of Brenth and I will gladly ride point for us." He kicked his horse a little to pass her, smiling at her as he rode past, closer than she would've liked.

He smelled of lilacs and fresh rain, an odd sensation to her, especially from a human. Most of them disdained the flowery scents of the elves, yet clearly this was a man of refined taste. Yet again her senses screamed warning; those were her favorite scents. When they stopped for the night, hours later as the goddess Silen rose high in the night sky, she settled in to *drift*, keeping her hand on Mithsran. Elves didn't sleep like humans did; instead they meditated on their lives and *drifted* back through their memories. This served to show them all their choices and to see what they had done, learning from their mistakes and relishing in their triumphs. Luckily it was a light meditation, and they could still hear what went on around them, so the man wouldn't surprise her if he tried something.

Her fears abated after the first two days of travel and she was smiling when they stopped in the city of Nalan, near the Amtar woods, and procured fresh horses. They stayed the night in the Wandering Unicorn Inn and exchanged stories that night while taking their meal in the common room. Shyi found herself talking easily with the man now, her former trepidations gone, and soon she excused herself to her room to drift.

RIKARD OF BRANTH SMILED as he watched the elven warrior walk away, not least because of the spectacular view she afforded while doing so. He patted the coin purse at his side, full of the gold cylinders Eliana Nightstar had paid him. Not that he needed much of a bribe to court the daughter of the noble house anyway, yet the money helped. He took another pull off of his mug and kicked his feet up, listening to the local bard play. He had been paid handsomely to watch her and bring her home, willingly of course. He was allowed to court the elven woman and to settle down in Tir-Onial as a smaller noble house under House Nightstar.

Rikard wasn't worried about the courting part; he was always the charmer with women of any race. No, it was the getting her home part that was the challenge, if he understood the warriors' motives well enough. He would have to appeal to her sense of family, and if nothing else, possibly cause a stir at home to send her running back. *I bet if there was an attempt on her mother's life that might send her running,* he thought, scanning the crowd. Sure enough, he found what he was looking for; a table full of less than reputable looking sell swords. They were everywhere of late, and could usually be bought for little coin. Rikard waited for them to leave and followed behind, hand on his massive sword.

As he exited the inn he heard a shuffling to his right and spun, pulling the chunk of steel off his back and parrying the smaller blade that flashed at him in the flickering torch light. The gasps of surprise that he stopped the blade came from all around him, and he took a club from behind, even as he sidestepped another attack. Swinging the large great sword in an arc, he heard the sound of snapping bone and the cry of pain from one of the men. "I have no desire to kill you all, gentlemen. I would just like to talk." He stood easily, not even breathing heavily as the four men stood around him, looking over their shoulders for signs of the guard. One of their number held his arm and slunk to the ground, the bone shattered and the cut deep through his leather armor.

"You have coin then?" The man speaking was the one with the smaller blade, one obviously trained in striking from the shadows.

"Oh yes gentlemen, and enough that you can even pay for your friends healing, I suspect." He smiled at them as he put his sword away, the huge blade slick with the man's fresh blood. "Now, let's walk and talk before anyone shows up to dissuade us." They followed him and soon he was back at the inn and sleeping peacefully, most of his coin gone. The news of the failed attempt on Lady Nightstar should reach them by the time they arrive at fort Nel'in and then they could race home. Rikard smiled at his devilish plan and looked forward to picking his new house name.

Chapter Four

Journey to the tower

Salen marveled at the speed of the river ship, it's odd design making it perfect for the trip up the River Shill. The river itself was wide, almost two miles across, and it's current this far down was strong. The *Mist Runner* was a wide ship, with an odd, white wood mast that seemed like it had been broken and fixed poorly, yet actually was made for a purpose, a purpose that would be needed as they neared the Southbridge. The white wood was Alin wood, a near unbreakable wood from the Alin tree found up north. It could only be harvested with magic, and even then, most elves wouldn't because they were so rare. The ships sails, made out of dark cloth, were full at the moment, Salen's magic propelling it faster than normal and the captain was furiously keeping up with the fighting current.

"Ready the mast Somrael!" the captain called out as he spun the wheel once more, the specially designed keel keeping them from tipping in the water as the boat turned against the fast moving water.

"Fra," Salen said once more focusing the winds through his stone and keeping the sails full. He was finally tiring, yet they needed the boost to get to the tower quickly. Once they were past the Southbridge he could let the normal winds carry them for a time. Most wizards could only focus so much of the energy of the world before resting, yet again, Salen was one of those rare wizards that could pull more than most. His record was ten castings straight, with prolonged concentration, before he blacked out. This was a record among wizards to this day only surpassed by archmages, and only a few at that, as most wizards could only handle five or six castings before the strain was too great. Even then, three or four made most wizards feel the effects and make subtle mistakes.

The Southbridge came into view and Salen smiled at the beauty of it. It stretched two miles across the raging river, its arc high enough for most lower craft and the beautiful stone supports leaving plenty of room for two ships to pass underneath at once. The *Mist Runner*, however, wasn't a low masted ship.

"Now Somrael!" Captain Greyson shouted as they fast approached the bridge.

Somrael pulled an iron pin out from the white mast and kicked it, the wind helping to fell the great beam. It was at least thirty feet tall and dropped to the bow like a stone, landing on the immense piles of hay situated there. The boat rocked, then steadied as they flew under the bridge, the mast sticking out like a knights lance. Once they were through the bridge, Somrael started to pull a rope around a great wheel and tie it off.

"Now crank that thing back up and we'll be in the final run," the captain said, smiling like the old adventurer he was.

Salen helped Somrael spin the crank, winding the rope around the sideways wheel and letting the crank do most of the work in hauling the mast back up. It was hard work, but after a couple of minutes, the captain ran over and set the iron pin in once more and whooped into the river spray as they bounced in the water. It was another two days to the tower, but the hard part was over, at least in theory.

THE NEXT DAY THEY WERE sailing through a very narrow channel just before the small fishing village of Heth when the lookout called out the colors of a ship. Salen heard the description, a white falcon on a grey flag, and frowned. The colors were from the far northern city of Khel'lis. "Captain, do not slow for that ship yet," Salen said as he walked to the bow and called for the power of sight upon the topaz on his anklet. It was the one stone he hadn't mastered yet and his magic was hit or miss with the physical stone. "Vew," he said, sending his eyesight out over the water and looking upon the incoming ship. "Oh crap." That was what he was afraid of...the people on the ship weren't from Khel'lis.

Khel'lis was famous for their hunters and most people from that city wore the same type of white fur cloaks. These cloaks were standard as the white ice wolf was one of the biggest problems in that area. Their pelts were used exclusively by sailors to keep the chill wind off during the winter months on the lake, and the people he saw on the ship weren't dressed in any of the usual cloaks. Also, the ship wasn't even Khel'lis born, as it had a deep keel and was suited for a more southern run near the deeper waters of the southern coast.

"Pirates then?" Somrael asked, already sliding his sword out and holding his necklace set with the jet stone.

"I'm almost certain of it," Salen replied, turning towards the captain. "They're not from Khel'lis."

"Right then, full sails ahead. Let's get out of this channel before they block us in," the captain ordered as the men scurried about the deck.

Salen turned once more and focused his will on the magic into the coral stone this time. "Wan," he called, pushing water towards the incoming ship with his will. It created a wave, that grew in size, which might give the *Mist Runner* time to get out of the channel.

"Well if they didn't know you were a talented wizard, they do now," Somrael said, laughing into the breeze. He held onto the rail as the *Mist Runner* banked hard, desperate to break free of the confining channel. There wasn't any room to maneuver if the ship came at them in here.

"That's why I haven't used my garnet stone yet...let them think I'm a novice." Salen laughed when the other ship's wizard broke the wave, waiting till the last minute and almost flooding the oncoming ship. *He isn't too good, or is he playing me like I'm playing him?*

"Almost out men, hold on!" the captain held fast to the wheel, the rudder protesting all the way. Considering how close they were to the shore, the boat may run aground before they clear the channel.

"Captain?" Somrael started to say, but was cut off by a stern look from the old veteran.

"We're fine. At this speed we'll push right through any ground we run into. Besides it's mostly sand at the end of this channel…I hope."

"He hopes?"

"You want to try sailing this thing, smart mouth?"

"Maybe I do!"

"Not now you two!" Salen shouted, trying not to laugh. He mentally sorted his stones and tried another tack with this unknown wizard. *Maybe a grand gesture then?* He looked over board at how shallow the water was and decided to try something different. *Well, when the dark one rides….* "Dir," he said, focusing his magic through the quartz and calling to the silt at the bottom of the channel. He felt the beginnings of strain as he cast for the third time in as many minutes and smiled as his arms went up and into fists; he could keep going for a while before he gave out, could the other wizard? The oncoming ship veered as a pillar of dirt and silt came up like a stalagmite, almost piercing the ship.

"Why didn't you do that sooner?" the captain asked, staring in wonder at the spectacle.

"That's why….Fra!" Salen said as he hastily threw up a shield of air as an incoming ball of fire roared at the ship. One would think you would use water as a shield, but it wasn't dense enough to stop the roaring mass of fire. Wind however could divert the projectile to the side and shield them from the concussive force. *That's four,* he thought as the ball of flame struck the water near the *Mist Runner* and exploded in a shower of water and steam. "I suggest you get this ship running, Captain."

"We're free!" The ship broke out of the channel and Thandyr turned the wheel violently, almost sending Somrael overboard.

The ship leaned dangerously close to tipping, but held as it banked around the oncoming ship. "Full sails men!"

Somrael held onto the railing for his life and gripped his jet tightly. "Mith!" he called to the forces and channeled them into his black stone. Shadows crawled up the side of the other ship and formed a haze of darkness to obscure their sight. "That ought to give us some room to run."

"Well done, friend," Salen said as he held onto a guide rope. He marveled at the ship's ability to turn like that and whistled as it righted once more, running freely. "Fra," he called to the wind, filling the sails again and sending the ship flying ahead. Salen looked back and frowned. He would like to go back and finish the fight with that wizard, but he had more pressing concerns at the moment. "Captain Greyson, I recommend hiring a competent wizard at the next port you find. Those pirates have themselves a good one and they seem to be doing very well for themselves out here."

"I shall indeed look into that. Thank Doral that you were here," Thandyr said, making the sign of the god of protection. It was customary to make the sign of the god you invoked, as if to honor their involvement, however slight.

"I'll handle the warding magic when we get close to the tower captain, but for now I'm going to go relax for a bit." Salen clapped the man on the shoulder and went below to grab a drink and *drift* for a bit.

THAT NIGHT AND THE next morning were spent quietly sailing on towards the island that held Lynn'el's tower. The ship slowed as they approached, all eyes were on Salen as he walked towards the bow. Swirling whirlpools dotted the edge of the island, preventing ships from getting too close without permission. He closed his eyes and called out to the forces around him, channeling them through the coral on his anklet. "Wan." The two whirlpools in front of the ship slowed and stopped, yet they wouldn't for long. "Go captain, I'll hold them until we're through," Salen said, beads of sweat forming on his brow already. Countering his master's spells wasn't easy, but he could do it at least; most apprentices couldn't claim that. The ship sailed through, the crew's eyes on Salen as they skirted disaster.

The island itself was beautiful, covered in short trees and bushes, with lush grass almost knee high. The small oaken dock was a welcome sight indeed to the weary sailors as they tied the ship up and weighed anchor. A crushed marble path led the way to the massive tower in the distance and Salen waved goodbye to the crew of the *Mist Runner* as he walked on. He would ask Lynn'el to cancel the whirlpools so the ship could depart for the southern city of Lyr'alan when he got to the tower.

"She's not going to mind that I'm with you is she?" Somrael asked as they walked the winding path.

"I don't mind a bit when the company is so handsome, young man." The voice was lyrical and flowing, like water over chimes. Lynn'el stepped out from seemingly nowhere, her smile wide and her arms spread to show no offense. She was short, barely five feet, and had long flowing white hair down her back. Tiny braids dangled in her weathered face as she walked towards them, her violet eyes sparkling in the warmth of Sulan's mid morning rays. Her robe was a deep azure, trimmed with gold and decorated with tiny pouches and gemstones and she carried a staff carved with runes that seemed to move with her every step. She held her age well and was still beautiful despite being one of the oldest elves still breathing.

"Master, I came as soon as I heard your message," Salen said as he bowed low, his hair sweeping low to the ground.

"Ever the charmer Salen. Come, introduce your fine young friend to me, apprentice." Lynn'el smiled and walked ahead of them, her staff tapping lightly as she walked.

"This is Somrael Anar, a fellow wizard of the shadows." Salen waved his hand in a flourish at his master and smiled. "Somrael, this is my master, the Archmage Lynn'el."

Somrael just stared, his mouth working silently. His hands went to three different pockets and he fumbled with his steps.

"I've never seen you this awkward in front of a lady, old friend," Salen said, laughing aloud.

"They've never been this beautiful," the dark-skinned wizard finally blurted out.

"Enough charm you two, an old elf like me can only take so much flattery." Lynn'el laughed and turned while walking, her steps never faltering. "We have much to discuss and none of it pleasant."

The tower itself was a small grey stone construct with a winding walkway leading up to a simple door. Their footfalls made no sound on the steps as they made their way up, and Lynn'el waved her hand at the door as they came closer, opening it with a thought. Soon they were sitting in comfy chairs with elven wine and fresh breads.

"So, dare I ask why I'm allowed here, Miss Lynn'el?" Somrael asked as she sat in a rather lavish chair, decanters floating around her pouring drinks by themselves.

"Oh pish, don't fret young half-elf, I don't stand on ceremony much, besides my apprentice will need help with what's happened." Her face grew serious as she sat back, sipping her wine and staring at Salen. "Ravin has escaped his confinement, my student, and all of Erendor is in trouble."

Salen swallowed his wine down the wrong pipe at the statement and coughed violently, gagging and spitting. "He what?"

"Wait, who is Ravin?" Somrael asked, sitting forward at the sudden tension in the room. "What am I missing?"

"You have not heard the tale of Ravin Dar and the battle that tore the land asunder?" Lynn'el asked incredulously. "The first of the human sorcerers that severed elven hands to work their dark magic?"

Somrael just stared at her, his mouth working silently. He sat back and drained his cup in one shot, closing his eyes and muttering to himself.

"Master, you have seen this?" Salen was composed once again; except for the wine stains on his white silk shirt, one would never know he had lost control at all. "Not that I doubt your power but..."

"You are right to ask, my student, and yes, I've seen the broken prison." She stood and walked over to a small pool of water held in a marble basin and took out a perfect sapphire gemstone. "I've had a ward on it since I confined him there all those years ago. It shattered the other day and I glimpsed the shattered rock opening for myself through this portal."

"Wait! Since you confined him?!" Somrael was on his feet now, his eyes wide.

"Yes dear, I'm just over eleven hundred years old," she said, laughing at his face as she sat down once more. "I was there on the Starmount and sent Ravin down into the molten rock we created to contain him."

Salen stood, dusting off the remaining droplets of wine from his longcoat. "So he'll be coming this way." It wasn't a question but a statement. "We'll go at once to the south and see if we can learn anything about his plans."

Lynn'el smiled and nodded, yet her tone grew grave as she crossed her legs and sipped more wine. "That was the idea my young one, however, heed my warning. The man is ancient and powerful. Do not attempt to cast against him unless you have no choice. He is far more powerful than most people ever gave him credit for."

"Don't worry master; after all, they say the same things about me." Salen bowed to her and grabbed Somrael's arm, dragging the dumbfounded wizard behind him. "Give us a good fifty heartbeats and lift the wards master, I'll send you a report as I can."

RAVIN STOOD IN THE center of the village, dressed in clothes a little too big for him, and smiled at the bodies that lay around him. The baron of Elenin, the quaint village he had entered that fateful night, had an impressive collection of rare stones. Most of them were worthless, except for the pure kyanite stone kept on his desk. Once Ravin had taken control of his mind as well, it didn't take long to order the extermination of the general populace. Now with the kyanite stone to focus the magic of spirit, he could raise the bodies of the dead villagers to be his distraction. Once he could get some more rest, and some more stones, he would make his journey to the resting place of the dragon.

They had laughed at him all those years ago when he had researched the dragons of myth. Dragons hadn't been seen for over a century back then, never mind in this day and age. He had questioned the baron before he killed him and it seems that they were still a myth, fairy tales in stories alone. He closed his eyes and focused the flow of magic from the hand of power out into the bodies around him, calling them to action. Yes, this time, no one would stand in the way of his raising the dragon and wreaking havoc upon the land.

Chapter Five
Collision Course

Shyi couldn't help but smile when she saw the wooden palisade walls of Fort Nel'in. This was it, the fate of all her training. She was going to join the ranks of the bravest warriors around Erendor and ride into battle across the countryside. Her blood pumping, she kicked her horse faster as they neared, galloping the last half mile to the fort. The wind whipped her white braids against her armor as she rode, the wind feeling like salvation to the woman who was always kept close by her family.

"In a hurry?" Rikard asked, pulling up next to her as his own horse fought to keep pace.

Shyi smiled even wider, her eyes gleaming in challenge. "Last one there takes care of both horses," she said, leaning down and urging her horse onwards with a quick squeeze of her knees and a snap of the reins. She pulled ahead and turned the last corner of the road, seeing the gate guard's panic and scramble their weapons up at the charging horses.

"You know they will impale us right?" Rikard shouted as he fell behind her white stallion.

"Feel free to slow down, stable boy!" Shyi whooped and turned her horse as they neared, coming right for the surprised guards who now had their pole arms planted in the dirt road to receive the charge. She caught Rikard's horse dropping back out of the corner of her eye, but it was too late to stop at this range. *Well, when the dark one rides...*

"Halt!" the readied guards shouted, clutching their weapons tight. The doors opened behind them as reinforcements came out, swords clearing their scabbards and shields being raised.

...You just hold on for your soul. Shyi held on as she gently squeezed her legs as they neared, jumping the horse clean over the guards. She had counted on them coming out to help and held her breath as the horse leapt up and over the pole arms, coming down hard inside the gate and kicking up dirt as she pulled hard to the right, trying to come around and slow down. Her armor took a sword swing on the side and another on the left leg before Rikard's voice shouted out over the tumult that they weren't enemies.

"Dismount and drop to your knees!" a rough voice called out, striding towards them. He had a blue plume on top of his helm and his sword had cleared his own scabbard as well.

"Captain, there's a second one out here." The guards called out as Shyi slid down off of her horse and held her hands up.

"We meant no offense, Captain. My name is Shyi..."

"To your knees!!" the captain roared, pointing his sword directly at her throat, cutting her off.

Shyi stared hard and squared her shoulders. "Not going to happen," she said, locking stares with the outraged captain. "And, if that sword draws blood, it will not be pleasant."

"Captain please, this is Lady Nightstar from Tir'Onial and we've come to join your ranks." Rikard's voice was pleading, as if they would actually kill them for this.

"You rush the gates and pull this stunt all to impress me?" the captain asked, some of his ire draining away.

Shyi shrugged her shoulders while keeping her hands up in the air. "Did it work?"

The captain dropped his sword and barked a laugh. "Well, send me to the flames it has." He gestured to the guards to let Rikard through and motioned her to drop her hands. "My name is Captain Lazzar, welcome to fort Nel'in."

SALEN STRODE FROM THE docks of Lyr'alan into the heart of the port city and took in the fresh sights of the marketplace. They had sailed for another day and paid captain Greyson another forty silver cylinders for his trouble, bidding him farewell for now. Now they were here in the port city of Lyr'alan to purchase horses and ride south towards Fort Nel'in to gather news of the wicked sorcerer and his movements.

"Salen, the stables are this way," Somrael said, stopping at the crossroads as the elven wizard kept walking.

"I'm aware, friend, but the market place is this way." He laughed and spun around, spinning his longcoat out as he did. "I love a good market place in the afternoon rays of Sulan's warmth."

Somrael shook his head and followed, catching up and patting Salen on the back. "You love a good marketplace full of women without their husbands."

"You're not wrong my friend," Salen said as they entered. It was a huge circle, with all roads leading towards this centralized meeting ground. Dozens of wagons, carts, and small shops lined the outer edge of the circle and still more blankets and barrels were situated in the inner circle where you could find more exquisite tastes like pipe weeds, fine drinks, and piercings. "Yet, I love browsing these markets for something even more coveted than lust." He channeled the forces of the mind through the jade on his anklet, whispering the word he needed. "Rule." His eyes glowed briefly as they adjusted to the power of objects around him, seeing if anything here was truly unique. Some of the long lost items created by archmages lost to the ages ended up in merchants' wagons as junk, their hidden power disguised to normal sight. Rusted rings, cracked swords and the like: You never knew what you may find in places like this. Salen walked the outer rings slowly, smiling at the pretty women that looked him up and down as he passed, always keeping his gaze out for that tell tale glow. Surprisingly enough he saw very few items, their faint glows nothing remarkable, until he got to the trappers cart.

This cart held furs and pelts of trapped and hunted animals that could be purchased for clothiers or hangings in the house. His gaze was drawn to a charred staff leaning against the back of the wagon, seemingly left alone and out of general sight. He never would've seen it if not for the massive glow coming off of it. "How much for the staff, good sir?" he asked, keeping his face calm and his voice bored.

"Staff? Oh my walking stick?" the man walked over and picked it up, looking at it and flaking ash off onto the packed earthen street. "This old thing?"

"Yes, I have a collection of things affected by nature and I have yet to find anything burned like that—still whole that is. I assume it was a fire that did that?" Salen leaned on the cart, keeping his tone even, lest the man sense urgency in his voice and think to charge him overmuch. He knew that staff was worth thousands, but he only had so much on him. Just another reason he was glad he didn't dress as a wizard; the man would know it was special if he was.

"Well, if it is that special I can let it go for say...fifty gold?" the man was almost drooling when he said it, thinking that he had some noble over a barrel.

Salen hemmed and hawed over the price for all of thirty seconds before standing up straight and shaking the man's hand. "Fifty? You, sir, have a deal." He pulled out his pouch and poured fifty gold cylinders in his hand, watching the man's eyes widen even more. He knew that only wizards used these for currency.

"Oh, I...I didn't know you was a wizard, good sir," the man said, trying to sound like he wasn't worried and failing miserably.

"The price is fair, have no fear. Only worry if you think to raise the price knowing my profession." Salen paid the man and took the staff before the man could argue, his slender elven hands wrapping around the unusually warm wood. It almost hummed when he touched it.

"It...It's never done that!" The man was backing away now, fear in his wide eyes.

"That's because you aren't a wizard." Salen planted the end on the ground and closed his eyes. *Oh yes, this thing is filled with power...what kind will take me some time, but it is an exquisite find.* He looked at the man again and smiled, "For your trouble, good sir," he said, handing the man a small token from his coat pocket.

"What is this for?"

"That is a pass for Tir-Onial's gates, waving the normal merchant fee. Use it if you ever bring your wares that way." He walked away without looking back, his mind once again on the journey at hand. "Let's get us some horses, Somrael, and see this fine countryside."

"Let us get some food and supplies before that so we don't starve as well."

"Great idea! You do that and I'll get the horses."

"I walked right into that, didn't I?"

"More like ran, but yes."

SHYI-LHANA RODE BEHIND the group of riders in her silver-chased armor sporting her new azure cloak. They had given her a test of battle, already passing her on the test of courage and welcomed her into the Riders of Erendor when she passed with flying colors. Rikard was tested as well and accepted, though they were less impressed with his entrance. Now they were heading out to an urgent call for help with six other Riders and she couldn't be happier. No parents to tell her who she should be, no nobility to say it wasn't acceptable, just a horse under her legs and a sword in her hand. Freedom.

"Nightstar, take point," Ride Commander Bellows said as he pulled back to the rear, "Blaesdan take center."

Shyi smiled at the name Rikard had to come up with on the spot. The riders didn't take warriors with no surname, so Rikard of Brenth became Rikard Blaesdan. She liked it, though it didn't seem to suit him for some reason. She urged her horse forward, replacing the point man and tightening her grip on Mithsran, her father's sword. They had ridden for five hours to the north of Fort Nel'in, searching for a large raiding party heading towards Lyr'alan. The captain had said that a messenger had come in exhausted, begging for help in stopping them. Now here they were and Shyi couldn't wait for her first battle as a Rider of Erendor. *You'll see mother, I'm born for this, not to be some wizard in a tower.*

"What brought you to the Riders, Shyi?" a young voice asked her, bringing her out of her reverie.

"What? Oh, well, I've always wanted to be a warrior and earn a reputation with my sword. My father said the Riders were looking for members so I figured it was a great place to start." She looked at the young man, accepted just three days before she arrived and smiled. Joras, she recalled. He had to be all of seventeen summers and awkward in his armor, but she had seen him with his short blade and he was focused. "What about you Joras?"

"Me? Oh, I want to see a real live dragon, just like in the stories." He sat a little straighter, like a brave warrior and made a sword salute like those storied knights.

Shyi laughed lightly with him until a harsh voice called out from behind them.

"Dragons are a myth Joras, quit daydreaming and pay attention." The man, Garor by name, was a brute, carrying a massive club on his back.

Joras frowned. "They haven't been seen in over a thousand years, 'tis true, but they did exist...they could come back."

"It's a fine reason as any Joras, never mind him," Shyi said, ignoring the brute and smiling at the young warrior. She was going to say more, but movement in the corner of her vision caused her to rein in and call a halt with an upraised fist, like they taught her. There, shambling across the field of high grass was a group of men heading north. They carried no weapons, yet something felt *wrong* about the look of them. One of their number, a man in the back, wore loose fitting clothes and carried some sort of rod. He alone turned towards them, as if he sensed them, and a chill rode down her spine.

"Stay here, lass," Garor said, pulling his club and riding ahead, "I'll see what this business is about."

"Commander, I don't like this," Shyi said quietly as the ride commander came up to her side at the front.

"You're new to us, Nightstar, Goror Everent is a capable fighter and can handle himself against any man." Commander Bellows smiled as they watched Goror ride up to the man in the rear, and lost that smile as the man pointed his rod at the Rider of Erendor with an almost lazy air and a lance of rock impaled both horse and rider from underneath, springing from the very earth below them. The screams of the horse, never mind Goror, echoed across the fields and the ring of steel from the remaining riders answered that attack.

"Stay with me, Shyi," Rikard said, coming up beside her horse as they charged the group. He had drawn his sword and had an unusual smile that almost said he was enjoying the man's death.

Shyi shivered and turned her focus towards the group, now seeing what was so wrong with them. As the group turned she could see that they were already dead, pieces falling off and huge cuts adorning their bodies that no living man could survive. Within seconds, the Riders of Erendor were in desperate trouble.

Chapter Six
The Rescue

Salen enjoyed the diminishing sunlight across the high grass plains, its rays the last light of the sun god's sight as it rested beyond the horizon and his sister Silen came up to the night sky. He rode casually, neither pressing the horses nor lollygagging. The plains were home to few predators, but there were some. His friend, Somrael, rode easily at his side, lost in thought as the favorite time of day came upon him. "What do you think the shadows will tell you this evening, old friend?" Salen asked.

"That's the best part of the shadows, you can never guess." Somrael worshiped the god Ta'ar, god of shadows and former lover of Silen. Kept apart because she was imprisoned in the night sky, he longs to find her and be with her once more. Or so the stories went. "But I hope tonight they impart some wisdom on how to fight an all powerful being."

"He's not all powerful, just extremely powerful." Salen corrected, and then stiffened as the horse under him grew agitated. He could feel the great beast tremble and fight his control, like it wanted to bolt. That usually happened when unnatural monsters were near. Not a good sign. "Swords out," he said, his own hand on his slim sword. Though he had his magic, he loved having a blade at the ready, it made him look dashing. A few minutes later, the sounds of battle became evident across the plains, carried on the chill wind of the evening. It was these sounds that also carried a whisper to them, the shadows calling them both.

"Oh that's not good," Somrael said as he listened intently to the language of his god. All true worshipers could understand the whispers of the shadows; it was something they learned to do when they accepted Ta'ar into their lives. "It says that fate lies ahead..."

"...and that it can't be evaded. I know I hear it too." Salen sat up straight and cleared his mind, focusing on the topaz on his anklet. "Vew," he said, channeling the power into the stone. This time however his imperfect control of the stone backfired and blasted back into him, almost throwing him from the horse. "Sorone, take it!" he swore, invoking the dark god's wrath. He still had yet to master the physical stone, the last before he could become an Archmage. His vision a little blurry, he kicked his horse into a gallop and chased the sounds of battle. "Looks like we ride in and get a surprise this night old friend."

SHYI-LHANA PARRIED another swipe of a rotted hand and spun away, bringing Mithsran around in an arc and severing the entire arm. The Riders had been decimated and the horses taken out quickly. Only her training and quick thinking had saved her and Joras from certain death as they engaged the enemy.

The dead felt no bite from steel, nor pain from clubs, clawing and biting anything that came at them with relentless fury. Commander Bellows had been lost, as well as two others, and now it was just her, Rikard, and Joras against a small gathering of the dead. The three fought back to back, defending each other as the group of more than twenty men came at them slowly but surely. Every time one was knocked back, it got back up in seconds to shamble at them.

"How can they keep coming without a head?" Joras asked, a hint of panic in his young voice. His short blade was soaked in gore, yet his arm was tired. "Shouldn't that stop them?"

"Stories again young one," Rikard said, shoving a body away and slicing at the leg to at least slow it down. "Bard's tales always say things like that."

"But how do they see us?"

Shyi frowned and looked at the man in the distance, smiling at their ineptitude. "He controls them with magic," she said, swinging again and sending another body tumbling away. She was conserving her energy using short precise attacks, and yet she was still tiring. She saw one stumble towards Joras and take the short blade without flinching, its fall unabated. "No!" she cried, as the young one went down under the weight of the man. Before she could lunge to his rescue, the body caught flame and burst in an explosion of gore.

"What!?" the man controlling the dead screamed, turning at two riders coming in fast.

Shyi looked at the two coming to her rescue and smiled, for the day was not lost yet. One of the riders, clearly an elf, was dressed in a long coat with a sword. He stood in the stirrups of his galloping horse with his hands outstretched as another body burst into flames. The other rode with his head down, clutching something at his neck and suddenly the man controlling these abominations was lost in a roiling darkness. She slashed out and ducked down, grabbing Joras and pulling him to his feet. "Stay with me Joras, we're not done yet." Shyi turned to Rikard just as the man took a massive fist to the side of the head from one of the dead and fell limp. "Gods in the sky, can nothing go right?"

His face burnt and tears streaking his face, the young man gritted his teeth against the pain and swung his blade, determination set in his blistered jaw. "I'll guard him, my lady. I'm with you till death now."

Shyi nodded and turned back to the dead, seeing them swivel as one to face the new threat riding towards them, yet they shambled aimlessly without vision to direct them. The elf on the horse motioned again, saying a word lost to her and split the ground between the dead, sending them tumbling as they rode right through them. He leapt off the horse and rolled, coming to a stop at Shyi's feet with a lopsided grin, covered in grass.

"Well hello there, fair maiden of the sword, fancy a rescue?" the elf said, getting to his feet with grace.

"I'm Shyi, this is Joras and Rikard, please tell me you can defeat that man and his warriors of death." She kept her sword at the ready as the other man rode up and dismounted, letting his horse run after the first one.

"So formal...My name is Salen and that is my friend, Somrael. And no, not if it is who I think it is, though I thought his choice in fashion would be better." The elf bowed low, swirling around and slashing the air with his sword for effect.

Great, a drama hound, she thought as they all heard a scream from the wavering darkness. A wave of earth picked them up and heaved, sending them sprawling and tumbling together. *"Fools!"* the man shouted, the darkness gone from around him. "Do you know whom you stand against?"

Somrael was the first to his feet, his hands drawing his own sword with a quickness befitting a warrior trained in battle. "Wait, Belin Waverly? Is that you? My old girlfriend from magic school?" he chuckled as he helped Salen up, then Joras. "I thought you gained some weight."

"Infidels! Quip all you want, but it will be your last." The man strode forward with such confidence that it caused most of them to take a step back...all but one.

Salen stood and took a breath. "Som, get them on the horses and ride for Lyr'alan." He muttered something else to himself and a wall of earth rose up around the man, then came crashing back down just as quickly. "Damn, this could take awhile."

"I'm not leaving you," Shyi said, pushing Joras towards the man called Somrael. "I'll stand with you against this foe or die trying."

"Gods in the sky, we have got to loosen you up woman," Salen said, turning towards the man again. "Fir," he said, causing the grass to ignite around the man. "This is a legendary sorcerer called Ravin Dar, and I can only keep him busy."

Shyi saw the fire go out as water appeared in the air and crashed down amid the flames. What worried her more was the fact that the group of dead men was still shambling north without direction...towards Lyr'alan. "We should try something he doesn't expect," she said, taking a deep breath and steeling herself. "Cover me."

Salen laughed. "Cover you? You realize this is a bad idea, right?"

"Good ideas are for old maids."

"Well said. Alright, I've got you."

Shyi ran headlong at the man, covering the distance quickly despite her armor. A fist of earth came out of the ground at her, but a wind blew her aside at the last minute, rolling her over and over.

"Sorry!" Salen called from behind her.

Shyi rolled to her feet as the air became colder around her. Hoarfrost started covering her armor and hands, the very moisture in the air freezing on her. She stumbled on, fighting the stiffness, then felt a warmth as her armor stated steaming, the silver metal heating up. She looked back at the elf and smiled, his eyes focused on her.

"You really do wish to die, don't you, young one?" Ravin asked as she closed the distance between them.

Shyi saw a severed hand in his grip as she got closer and real fear crawled up her spine and kicked her brain. *I just charged a sorcerer with only a sword,* she thought as she kept going. Not much else to do now that she had gotten this far. That was the dangerous thing about human sorcerers, they never tired of pulling the forces around them. Since it was channeled through the elven hand, they ignored the strain of magic that every wizard felt. They could literally cast all day long. Then she had an idea. *What's the worst that could happen? Oh yeah, death...*

RAVIN COULD NOT BELIEVE what was happening. It had all started so well, raising the dead with his new stone and marching north. Then the troublesome Riders of Erendor showed up and he had some fun destroying them utterly with his new playthings. Bodies raised by spirit but devoid of a soul were completely under your control and, gods in the sky, did he enjoy that, yet the elven female and her companions would not succumb. When he saw the elf he thought to see some magic, but she just fought like a warrior and watched her friends fall around her.

Then that true wizard showed up on horseback and ruined his day. Now he had a fight on his hands. Oh, he wasn't taxed by any means, though the elf could sling spells with the best of them. No, but the elven woman was coming at him, protected by the wizard! He threw earth at her and even water, trying to freeze her, to no avail. If he had all of his stones they would be dead right now, but he only had a limited selection. "You can't win against me," he said to the oncoming warrior, her sword raised above her head in typical barbaric fashion. "Once I raise the dragon, I will destroy you all!"

Ravin knew these warriors and their pride. She would try to cleave him in two, but his magic would take her before that. "Loktar," he whispered, sending the magic through the hand and into her mind. *Counter that wizard*, he thought, yet noticed her eyes weren't glazing over. It was then he saw what she was wielding, the very sword that had helped stop him all those centuries ago... except, to him, it was yesterday. Mithsran, the sword of shadows. It protected its wielder from the darkest parts of their own mind, and made them immune to control. He gritted his teeth and waited until the last moment, knowing if he cast too soon, the other elf would try and counter. As she came at him, he sent a lance of earth at her head, blocking her swing and taking her out of the fight. Except, he missed.

He heard the clang of metal and thought he got her, but she ducked at the last minute, letting go of her weapon. The powerful warrior shouldered into him at speed, cracking his ribs and sending them to the ground in a tumble. Punches, kicks, and head butts flew into him, his blood smearing her armor. He was too weak to fight her off, only having been free for five days. In the end she had him down and her foot on his throat, unable to speak the commands to use magic. Before he could tell them of the uselessness of killing him, the elven wizard stepped up and stabbed him in the heart.

"Now, let's ride after those dead men and make sure they never reach Lyr'alan." This from the one that shrouded him in darkness: another wizard, yet a mongrel.

"Wait, we can't let him keep this hand..." The elven woman was there again, reaching for his Hand of power.

The elven wizard barred her way. "I wouldn't touch that my lady, 'tis a cursed thing and has to be dealt with a certain way and I know not what that will be." He walked her away, his arm around her protectively. "Archmage Lynn'el will know. Now let's be off, but we're sticking together — after all I have to teach this lady to relax a little." He flourished his long coat like some fancy noble at a party and walked away. It was then that Ravin saw the anklet around the elven wizard's leg and knew that he had faced someone of power. The last thing he heard was them all walking away, discussing how to stop him when he got up.

Chapter Seven
Complications

Rikard had a terrible headache and his scowl wasn't helping. He'd been holding this particular scowl for the last ten miles, ever since he was introduced to the newcomers. The dark skinned half-elf was a mongrel, and the wizard was entirely too cheerful; he didn't trust them one bit. It didn't help that the woman that was going to get him his own title was staring at the handsome wizard the entire ride. "Why are we riding all the way around the dead again?" he asked, even though no one was paying him any attention.

The elven wizard, Salen, turned in his saddle and smiled that annoying smile. "Because if we hit them from the front, at a good distance, we can take more of them without getting punched in the head."

Rikard shot Joras a deadly look when the young rider snickered but otherwise conceded to the wizards thinking. "How much longer do you think it will take to get near Lyr'alan and head back in front of them?"

"We should start to turn west any minute now, then it will only take another hour to see them coming." The wizard turned back and whispered another word of magic, his eyes focused far away.

"Can't you just burn them all in one great blast, Sir Salen?" Joras asked, clearly in awe of their rescuers.

"First, he hates being called sir," Somrael said, clapping the young rider on the shoulder as he rode next to him. "Second, he could but it may well ignite the entire plain on fire. Before you ask — yes he could just put it out, but being reckless with magic always leads to unforeseen consequences."

"So, basically, we're going to watch you pick them off one at a time and feign interest?" Rikard was trying not to sound like he would rather eat his socks boiled with his long shorts, but he failed horribly.

Salen smiled as he canceled his magic and shook his long white hair. He seemed completely unfazed by the remarks and laughed at it like it was a joke. "Fear not, brave rider of Erendor, you don't have to feign interest with me. I'll kill them whether you care or not."

Rikard frowned and rode on in silence, wondering if his well paid mercenaries had absconded with his money without doing the job. He should've been alerted to any attack on house Nightstar by now, especially with Shyi's mother being a high ranking wizard.

IT WAS NEAR DUSK WHEN Salen stood among the bodies of the dead, his magic still pulsing through some of them as they twitched on the ground among the high grass. In the end, the others did use swords, but only because they were bored and wanted to do something besides watch him trounce the dead with magic. It was Joras that first spotted the riders coming in from the west, and at great speed.

"Somrael, it's too dark for me, can you see their colors?" Salen asked, wiping imaginary dirt off of his longcoat.

Somrael pulled his necklace out and murmured the word to see in gloom and focused on them. "It looks like stars around a sword...field of dark blue maybe?"

"That's house Nightstar!" Shyi exclaimed, worry creeping into her voice.

"Hail the riders!" Rikard shouted as they neared, startling them into pulling their weapons in the deepening gloom. Once they saw the group however, they sheathed them and made way for a rider in black. It was Marcus Keller, the lord high commander of Tir-Onial himself.

"Lady Nightstar, you must ride with us at once for the capitol," the man said, his voice low and halting, as if emotion ruled his words.

Salen frowned and stepped forward, knowing the gravity of his words. He had heard that tone before and knew what was coming. "Lord high commander, we are weary from battle with the dead and have need of rest, shall we not go to Lyr'alan for the night and speak over a mug of ale?"

"Ah, Wizard Valari, I didn't recognize you without your robes." The commander lowered his head and sighed. "Sadly no, we cannot. The news is grave indeed and the Lady Nightstar needs to ride to the city with haste before the council deteriorates into endless bickering."

"You keep calling me 'Lady' good sir, yet that title is reserved for my mother as you well know. Now I ask you in seriousness sir...what is going on?" Shyi stood trembling yet resolute, her back straight even through the fear radiating out from her.

"Very well Lady. There has been an attack on the Nightstar Villa and both your father and mother have been killed. You are the heir to the Nightstar house and the seat on the council." Tears fell silently down his dirt covered face, his leathers likewise stained by his road weary travels; they must've ridden night and day to get here. "You have my sincere condolences on this tragedy."

Salen moved quickly as she fell backwards, catching her in his arms and lowering her to the ground as she wept, her anguished cries a reminder of his own when the commander had told him of his own parents' deaths. "I've got you...it's going to be alright." He focused his magic into the jade on his anklet and whispered the word to ease her mind into sleep. "Doz."

"How did this happen?" Rikard seemed furious, stomping forward and eliciting the guards to once again draw their weapons. The warrior stopped and clenched his fists at his sides. "Lady Nightstar was a powerful wizard, what manner of thug could best her?"

As the beautiful lady warrior fell asleep in his arms, something in the man's voice drew Salen's gaze and he narrowed his eyes as the man stood there and blustered at the commander. "You said that both Lord and Lady Nightstar were killed, lord?" Salen asked, gently laying Shyi on the grass and motioning for Joras to watch her. He walked forward and circled Rikard as he asked. "Commander, how were they slain if I may ask?"

"They were cut down with blades. It seems they were in their garden when they were attacked."

"Well, my friend here is right about two things it seems. There should be no way they should've slain her with the magic she could wield." Salen patted Rikard on the shoulder and walked away, silently vowing to keep an eye on this one.

"What was the second thing?" Rikard asked as he turned away from the commander.

"What now?"

"What was the second thing I was right about?"

"Oh, well, somehow you knew who, or should I say what, attacked the Lady Nightstar." Salen bowed to the warrior mockingly. "I have underestimated your powers of deduction in this area, good sir. I, myself, had assumed that she would've been attacked by a wizard and bested, yet you guessed that it was a...thug? Is that what you called them?"

Somrael walked forward and clapped Salen on the shoulder, a solemn look on his face. "Lucky guess then old friend, let us gather the lady and ride for the city. We can discuss this at a later date."

"Assuredly." Salen blocked Rikard from going to Shyi with an arm and scooped her up himself. "Joras, guide the lady's horse would you?" He placed the elven warrior on his own horse and leapt into the saddle. "Lead the way commander."

RAVIN STOOD ON THE plains of high grass and watched them ride away west and smiled. They may have defeated his distraction, yet he had a new plan now. That bothersome wizard had said a name that was very familiar to him, and it was time to pay an old friend a visit. The sorcerer started walking north towards the city lights in the distance and vowed that this time he would see Lynn'el fall by his hand. *Or rather this hand,* he thought as he shook the severed elven hand like a celebratory streamer. He laughed aloud at his own joke and, within the hour, was striding towards the closed gate of the city.

"Hail the traveler," a voice called out from the torch lit gate, no one in direct view.

"Greetings good man, may I enter your fair city and find shelter and food for the evening?" Ravin asked, knowing that he had to play nice at least for now. Once he completed his goal and called the dragon to his side, then all of this would be in flames.

"You travel afoot with no belongings?" The guard's voice was wary, yet soft. Real compassion was found in most people, you just had to exploit it.

"Yes, alas, my companions and I were beset by brigands; I, alone, survived to tell the tale." The lie came easily and soon the gates were creaking open, two guards with a blanket and torches came for him. They looked him over and saw the bruises and scrapes that were already healing from his altercations with those heroes.

"Here, the Lucky Wyvern is the best in the city," the guard said, pressing a gold coin into Ravin's hand. "Take this and get some hot stew and bread. Tell the Goodwoman, Linna, that Baren sent you and you will have the best room as well."

"Many thanks, good sir, might I also ask if there is a merchants bazaar here in the city?" Ravin needed to replenish his stones and if he could fill out the rest, then that old archmage would indeed beg for her life.

"Lyr'alan boasts the best around the lake and tomorrow is the first of the season so they will have full carts as well." The guard nodded to him and they closed the gate.

Ravin went on his way, taking care to limp slightly until out of sight. *First of the season indeed,* he thought as he strolled down the street and looked around at the city. It was large and he vaguely remembered the name from his time all those centuries ago. Back then it was an elven port town named Lyr, known for its massive docks and deep waters near the shore. Yes, this would be perfect for his needs and soon he would resume his travels to the far northern mountains and his destiny.

Chapter Eight
Traitor

Shyi walked into the garden woodenly, stiff from grief and riding all night long. She was asleep for a good part of the ride, but that didn't help; her dreams punished her just as much as reality had. Her eyes were swollen and red, puffed up from crying, and her joints ached. While a part of her refused to believe that they were gone, she could feel the hole in her heart as soon as she stepped inside of her home. The wind howled its own lament as she entered their final resting place, the bodies kept there until she arrived, preserved by magic from the wizards of the city.

A comforting arm reminded her she wasn't alone, the elven wizard in the longcoat still by her side. Salen had been a blessing through this, explaining that he had lost his own parents as well and offering to listen whenever she could finally digest the horrific scene; he knew what was coming. The others were here as well, not that she could get rid of Joras now if she wanted to; the young rider had pledged his life for her. She turned the last corner of the winding path and beheld her worst nightmares. Even knowing what she was going to see, the sight still took her breath away. Lying together, shielding each other from harm, were the bodies of her parents. Stifling a sob, she tried to go to them, but she couldn't...her legs giving out and crumpling to the dirt floor. The grass around them was burned away to bare earth and they showed no signs of fighting back, only huddling together.

"Where are the bodies of the attackers?" Rikard asked, his voice echoing in the solemn quiet of the garden. He was met only with stares of varying anger and open contempt.

Shyi saw that they were holding hands, and noticed that her mother wasn't wearing her council ring. "Where is my mother's ring?" Shyi croaked out through her tears. *Oh father...mother, what have I done?* Her thoughts were dark this day and indeed were that way ever since hearing the news; she knew they had died because she had left. She couldn't understand how she knew this, only that it was a fact...somehow.

"It was found on her nightstand, Lady Nightstar." The man speaking now was the official investigator, the lord high commander retiring to his chamber to rest after the long ride both ways. He turned towards Rikard and regarded him coldly. "As for the attackers, they were taken away and the survivor questioned."

"Survivor?" Rikard asked, a tremble in his voice.

"I want him brought here now," Shyi said, her voice turning to steel in a second.

"I don't think that's..."

"Stop." Her voice was unforgiving and held no room for argument. "Look at the way they sit." Shyi pointed to the bodies of her parents as tears still fell. "What do you see?"

The investigator stood straighter and frowned. "What we wrote in our report lady. That they were taken unawares and in a moment of reflection...obviously."

Salen laughed, then covered his mouth, wincing. "Sorry, that was just funny."

Rikard rounded on the wizard, fury in his eyes, shouting in the elf's face. "And just what is so funny about their death!?"

Salen went from laughing to dead serious in a heartbeat, his eyes almost flames as he looked up at the warrior standing in front of him. "If you shout in my face like that once more, dear Rikard, you will never shout again. Do I make myself clear?"

Somrael broke them up, laughing nervously. "Yes, yes, but he has a good question this time. What is so funny, Salen?"

"The fact that a wizard as talented as the former Lady Nightstar was taken *unawares*," he said, turning towards Shyi. "You see it too, don't you?"

The investigator was at a loss. "I don't see the point..." he looked at Shyi and nodded. "What do you see, good lady?"

Shyi sighed and looked at Salen with respect. He had seen the truth without knowing them as well as she did, the wizard was good indeed. "My mother's ring was left inside, and they are holding hands...something they haven't done in over twenty years. We had a terrible fight when I left and it split them apart." Her eyes filled with tears once more, but she steeled herself to continue. "They never saw their attackers because they were drifting together."

"But isn't drifting a light rest?" Joras asked quietly from the back.

"Normally yes, but when two elves join in the drift, especially if they are life mated, they share each other's memories and go deeper than normal," Salen answered, stepping forward and taking a pinch of dirt in his fingers. He whispered something and sniffed it, coughing a second later and smiling. He nodded to the investigator as if he had known what he would find. "Life fire, I suspected as much when I saw the pattern."

The investigator knelt down as well, taking a sample and putting it in a pouch. "Yes, astounding in and of itself. She burned them all to a crisp within seconds with her own life force, never channeling it through any stones we could find near her. She had left them inside as well."

"Exactly, so they had no idea that there was anyone here. That means someone paid good money for this. Money that they used to buy protection to get past her wards." Shyi turned towards the investigator once more. "Now, do what I say and bring him to *me*!"

Salen stood as the man scurried off, and took Shyi's hand. "I'm sorry about your parents; know that they shared the best memories of you in their last moments."

"And just how would you know that?" Rikard asked, snorting his displeasure.

Salen smiled at the female warrior and closed his eyes. "I really may kill him before too long." He turned before she could say anything and pointed straight down to the scorched earth. "Because of that."

Rikard waited, staring at the dirt then back to the wizard. After an uncomfortable silence and some giggling from Somrael, he gave up and stalked towards Salen once more, stopping before he could come within sword reach. "Are you going to tell us?"

"Tell you what?"

"How you know that?"

"I did, you just don't understand the answer."

"For the love of Doral, answer the question so we can understand it!" Rikard was on edge, which was clear to them all. Why, though, was anyone's guess.

Shyi knew that the wizard was being curt and sarcastic just to goad the man, yet she too wanted to know. Luckily she had dealt with wizards like this before. "Tell us, grand wizard, what gave away the fact that they were thinking of me?" Laying her hand on his arm, in that moment, caused a spark to jolt through them.

"Of course, my dear. Not only is Life fire extremely tricky to control, it also takes on the form of the last thing they were thinking about." He pointed to the ground again and when everyone still looked skeptical he sighed and walked up the path towards the house. Once up by the door he climbed the tree and beckoned her.

Shyi smiled, and walked up, shocked that he chose her favorite tree. *Coincidence again? Or is this another sign?* She banished her thoughts and climbed up next to him, gasping at what she saw below. There, in the dirt, was a clear pattern, an outline that was unmistakably her face! She turned towards him and in the tight space in the tree their faces were inches apart. The electricity was evident to them both and she was just seconds from kissing him when the investigator came in. "Am I the only one that feels that?" she asked breathlessly.

"It's a little hard to ignore being this close," Salen said as they stared into each other's eyes.

Shyi looked away first, the eyes of the wizard almost too much even for a seasoned elven warrior as herself. Something about how they seared into her soul made her feel vulnerable... a feeling she usually avoided at all costs. "Let's get down there and talk to this thug."

"Another time then," Salen said, as if he knew they would have more time to figure out this feeling.

RIKARD WAS IN TROUBLE and he didn't see a way out. He was horrified when he realized his money paid for the deaths of Shyi's parents and now that there was a survivor... well it could end badly for him. He had taken his frustrations out on the small elven wizard, yet the powerful elf had stood up to him with a fire inside those eyes that he honestly didn't want to tangle with. The dark skinned mongrel was lurking in the back of the garden now, looking for other clues as to how things transpired and the young Joras was guarding the door like a faithful lapdog. *How am I going to silence this guy before he tells them I was the one that hired him?* His thoughts came crashing to a halt as he saw Shyi climb the tree after the wizard.

All of his plans were crumbling to ash and his eyes narrowed as he saw them sitting close on the branch, their chemistry evident to everyone looking at them. With the death of Eliana Nightstar, his dreams of marrying into nobility were washing away like a boat in a storm. Then the investigator came in with the prisoner and Rikard knew that if he didn't come up with something quick, his dreams of being alive would quickly follow. His eyes darted to Somrael, who was busy looking at the garden wall, then back to Salen and Shyi, who seemed like they were getting a little too friendly. That left Joras as the only one who could stop him. He strode towards the entrance, his hand on the massive blade on his back.

Rikard was no novice with a blade; he had trained for years to be the best in Branth and beyond. He had even trained with an elven blademaster when he arrived at Tir-Onial, but soon left on his errand for House Nightstar. As he moved towards the investigator he moved his eyes to Joras and widened them. "Joras, what are you doing?" He drew his sword and swung a wide arc around the prisoner, aimed at the young rider. Joras stepped back, drawing his own sword in shock, yet there was no way he could stop that massive blade. Rikard pulled his swing short and feigned the block anyway, giving Joras the perfect time to strike.

Rikard watched the shock give way to determination and the young rider lunged, the perfect opening too good to pass up. Rikard backed up perfectly and let the sword come, knowing where the blade would hit. As the blade penetrated his midsection, Rikard gripped the blade and pulled harder, pushing it all the way through and into the prisoner. When he heard the soft gasp from behind him, he swung his massive blade again, this time with his full force. The young rider's head bounced along the garden path as the great sword clanged to the walkway.

He heard the commotion of those around him and smiled, knowing that the prisoner was already wounded by the fight with Eliana and probably would bleed out here before they healed him. Of course he was counting on Salen healing him over the prisoner, but that would only work if his ruse had succeeded. Now it would look like he was only trying to protect the man he had hired in the first place and no one would be the wiser. As darkness took him, he heard Shyi beg for Salen to heal him and he slipped into that formless void already planning his wedding to the female elven warrior. *She will be mine...*

Chapter Nine
End game

It was three days later when Salen stormed out of the wizard's school, frustration on his furrowed brow. After they had laid the Nightstars to rest and mourned their loss, he had spent a full day cloistered with the other wizards and archmages, describing the sorcerer they had faced and his plans on raising a dragon. They had done everything short of laugh at him, dismissing him out of hand and calling the story a delusion. Their arguments went round in his mind as he thought furiously what his next steps were to be.

"A dragon caller, as you have described this supposed sorcerer, is only a myth, as are dragons," one mage had argued.

"The power needed to actually call a dragon from its slumber and command it would be phenomenal," another wizard almost yelled from his seat.

"Never mind the fact that the man you say is doing this was slain over nine hundred years ago," the arch mage Ellerian said in finality. *"Take these words to your master Lynn'el and tell her that we wish to speak to her about placing these notions in your head."*

"I'm guessing that it didn't go well?" Somrael asked, coming out of the shadows of the nearby alley and stepping in rhythm with his friend.

"Your gift for understatement should qualify you for Archmage status, dear friend." Salen laughed despite the failure of his warnings and felt a little better. His friend always knew how to bring him out of his moods.

"Speaking of that....How goes the mastery of your last stone?" It was a touchy subject, yet Somrael broached it often.

"Not well, I'm afraid. The topaz resists all attempts to master it, almost teasing me with its power. I know I have to force it, yet something holds me back." Salen could still use it, but the spells backfired every once in a while. He needed a task that could make the stone see that he was in charge, and nothing had made itself clear to him as yet.

Mastery of stones was different for each wizard attempting them, the trails suited to their unique signatures. Some wizards mastered stones simply by using them in ways they've never thought of, other wizards master them by monumental tasks, pouring everything they have into the casting of spells, yet others master stones without trying; It was all up to the magic.

"Don't look now but your sweetie is coming," Somrael said, punching him in the shoulder.

Salen ignored the remark with practiced ease and frowned at the man striding alongside the elven warrior. Rikard had saved the day by killing the traitor, yet something didn't sit right with him about it all. He had healed the man on Shyi's urgency, yet even though the facts laid out in front of him said it was cut and dry, there was something off about the entire thing. *That young rider just didn't have it in him to try something like that.* Sadly, even he knew that without anything to go on it would seem like a jealous rivalry. So he let it go, yet he was going to keep his eyes on the massive warrior and his hunk of steel he called a sword.

Shyi waved and hurried to them, her smile like a ray of sunshine from Sulan himself. "Hey there, you two."

Salen was about to say something witty and cutting, flattering her figure and insulting Rikard when a pain lanced through his mind, blocking out his vision and dropping him to the cobblestone road. A voice came to him then from far away: the voice of his master Lynn'el.

Salen, ware the Dragon caller. He is here in his full power and I cannot best him. Though he may slay me, know that he can be fought and brought down by that which he thinks is his greatest strength. Her words were faint, as if strained from battle and distance. *You have greatness in you and it will shine when you need it most. Fare well student, you have my eternal love and warmth.*

"No! Lynn'el!" Salen screamed from his knees on the stone street. His friends were upon him, urgency in their voices. He blocked them all out, focusing on his master's voice and following it back on the very magic she was using to go to him, while the connection was still up. He had only read about this in the oldest tomes and scrolls and the wizards today swore it was all fables and fairy tales; still he had to try and get to her.

No Salen...it is too...aaahhhh!

Salen was out of time. "Gra eu car'cen!" he called to the magic, forcing it through the topaz and kyanite stones simultaneously without even thinking of failure. He was going to physically follow the trail to his mind backwards and use spirit to anchor him as he went. At the last moment, Shyi and Rikard grabbed him and he knew he had to pour more of himself into the magic lest they become lost along the way. The magic swirled around and suddenly they were gone, the street empty except for Somrael and the stares of the people that witnessed it all.

COLD STONE UNDER HIS knees brought Salen out of his stupor just as his master screamed and collapsed, her burnt form turning to ash as it hit the floor. His eyes snapped open as Shyi and Rikard staggered away from him, smashing into the tables and racks of his master's laboratory. Ravin stood there, flames wreathed around his hands, a gleam in his wild eyes. Before Salen could think of what to cast, a loud chime echoed throughout the chamber. It came from his anklet, which was now glowing brightly, stunning everyone. He had finally mastered the topaz. *No time to dwell on the implications of that now,* he thought as he stood defiantly, ready to burn the tower down to avenge his master. He pulled his new staff out in his off hand and wondered if it would help him this day.

"What is this!?" Ravin called out, clearly shocked at the arrival of people out of thin air. He looked down at the ashes at his feet as if this was some sort of trick, then back at the trio in front of him. "Do you think you can best me, young one?" he sneered, stepping back and readying himself. "I am a dragon caller and I won't be denied."

"No I do not, yet I am going to try anyway," Salen answered smiling. He could tell his master's wards were still up as he still couldn't lie in here. Lynn'el had some weird spells cast around her tower and one of her strict rules were no lies when working magic with her. Results could be catastrophic if you weren't ready for the magic. You had to be honest with yourself as well as the people around you when working with magic in close quarters like this.

Rikard recovered first and stumbled forward, drawing his huge lump of steal he called a sword. "I've invested too much in my future to die here," the warrior began, his eyes narrowed at the sorcerer. "There must be something we can work out so the lady and I can go free?" He looked shocked, realizing he couldn't stop himself.

Ravin laughed as he raised a shield of air, whirling around himself and scattering scrolls around the room... at least the scrolls that hadn't already been burned up in the last fight. "Fine with me. Kill the wizard and I will let you both walk free."

Shyi drew her own sword and turned towards Rikard, astonishment written all over her visage. "What are you doing Rikard?"

"Anything I can to make sure that I get what your mother promised me!" he said, struggling not to talk now.

Salen called up his own shield, a revolving wall of both water and air. He circled Ravin and looked for hints as to what the ancient sorcerer would lead as his companions stared each other down. He kept a solid eye on Rikard as well, not trusting the man as far as he could throw him. Lynn'el's truth spell was having some interesting effects; that could mean he would be fighting on two fronts. Might as well play both fights at the same time while he could. "Let me guess Riakrd... she promised you her daughter?"

"Yes, and a title. I just had to get her home. That's why I..." he snapped his mouth shut as he trembled against the magic, bringing his sword to bear on Salen while stepping away from Shyi's reach.

"Why you what?" Shyi lunged with her sword, knocking his heavy blade up away from Salen and interposing herself in-between them. "What did you *do?*"

"They were only supposed to hurt your mother...not kill her!" Rikard blurted out, unable to resist the magic of the archmage that wove the wards. He blocked her next three attacks, backing away from the furious elven warrior.

Ravin whispered and held up the elven hand, its fingers holding a myriad of gems at once. Flames rose from his hands and snaked through the air at Salen slowly, like they were testing his defenses. "I've been casting all day young wizard, can you say the same?"

"I just pulled off a translocation spell with passengers and didn't break a sweat...what do you think old man?" he smiled as he realized that actually shocked the sorcerer, then he remembered his anklet. "Oh and its Archmage now. Dir!" Salen stomped his foot and called to the earth under the tower, shaking the entire structure and throwing them all off balance, pulling his slim sword and slashing at the man's shield to no avail. He had to keep the man off balance if he was to have any chance at all in these close quarters. Shyi and Rikard went blade to blade in the background as he advanced once more on the sorcerer and that gave him an idea.

Salen used his new staff to absorb the incoming fire tails and marveled at how solid this charred staff felt in his steady hands. He cast a water spell to sweep Ravin's legs and waited for the man to counter as he moved towards Shyi once more "Shyi, swing at Rikard's feet."

"What? Why?" She blocked another lazy swing by the man and fought back twice as hard.

"Trust me." Salen maneuvered Ravin in front of the door to the room and waited.

Shyi ducked low, against all her instincts, and swung for Rikard's legs. Predictably, he switched his grip to a two handed over head swing and brought his sword down at her. She threw up her sword but there was no way to deflect it, only take the brunt of the attack and absorb the shock and weight.

Salen knew it wouldn't kill her, though she wouldn't be able to recover from it... but that wasn't the point. He had to time this perfectly or they would all be dead. He ducked quickly shouting to the peridot stone on his glowing anklet as he spun and pushed Shyi's head down lower. "Sho!"

Rikard swung down and was hit by the gust of wind, sending him over the two huddled elves and into Ravin's shield. The mass of heavy steel and the man's strength behind it cut right through the wind and into Ravin's shoulder. The force of the wind-assisted blow hurled them both out of the room and tumbling down the stairs of the tower, giving Salen time to think.

"What do we do?" Shyi asked, standing awkwardly and looking at the door. A simmering anger was just underneath her skin and her hands were trembling.

"Sadly, I think we need to flee." Salen stood and looked around for anything salvageable, grabbing some scrolls and stones; then his eyes saw the pouch on his master's table. It was her favorite one, the one that held her most precious stones and he knew she would never use them again. He scooped it up and looked at the window. "Let's go, before they get up." He grabbed Shyi's hand and called to the wind as he climbed out of the window and jumped. He would regroup and chase this guy down, hopefully before it was too late.

RAVIN STOOD SLOWLY, blood pouring down his ruined arm. He called to the kyanite in the hand and slowly stopped the bleeding as he walked back up the stairs, stepping over the unconscious man with the massive sword. He would've healed in time, but this was quicker. That wizard, no, Archmage, had appeared in an instant from somewhere else. This was something that his old colleagues had only guessed at and never thought possible, yet he had seen it with his own eyes. A formidable opponent to be sure, but one he could deal with later. First, he had a dragon to raise.

"Up, imbecile, we have work to do." Ravin said, kicking the man that had almost killed him. If he had been a foot to the left it would all be over right now. That archmage was good at thinking on his feet.

Rikard came to with a gasp, scrambling back and looking for his weapon. "You...what?"

"Your companions are quite upset with you, but I think that could work for me. Follow me on a little errand and I promise to give you what you desire." By the time he walked back up to the top of the stairs, his arm was almost fixed.

"Are you really going to call up something from the old stories?" Rikard asked, sheathing his sword on his back and following.

"I really am. I have a boat waiting for us down by the docks that will take us north. Let us go and embrace destiny as I should've all those years ago."

Epilogue
Bedtime

He closed the book as Nivia sat up, the covers falling to the bare floor. He knew she would be cross, yet her reaction still surprised him.

"Uncle, that can't be how it ends!" Nivia crossed her arms and pouted, her displeasure reminding him she was of his blood after all. "You can't end a story like that!"

"Relax child, there is a bit more to the story but I promised your mother that if it was late I would hold off on the ending for fear of nightmares." He had to laugh at her outrage; she seemed way too small to hold that kind of temper.

"Please Uncle? I can't sleep without knowing the ending."

"Very well, but remember that this is only book one after all," he said with a stern wave of his hand as she sat back and dragged the covers off of the floor once more. "You will really have to wait a couple more months for me to visit again for the second part."

"I understand, Uncle...I'll be patient after this...I swear."

"Very well, a promise is a binding thing after all; stronger than most magics in these stories." He sat back and opened the book to the last pages once more, clearing his throat and waiting for her to be comfortable again. "They had escaped, yet where could they truly go?"

THEY HAD ESCAPED, YET where could they truly go? Salen and Shyi ran for the far side of the small island, away from the docks where Ravin surely had enthralled slaves waiting for him. Salen was depleted from the mastery of the topaz, never mind the spell battle with an ancient sorcerer. They stole down to the water's edge and found Lynn'el's private sailboat, taking it and making for Lyr'alan as fast as Salen's magic could whisk them there. Shyi was withdrawn and in shock, finding out that one of her close friends had been a part of her parents' death, never mind had tried to sell them out. It was a day and a half before they pulled into the docks of the large town, and they had just tied the boat up when the first screams came from behind them.

People were pointing to the far northern sky and calling out for the gods to save them, cowering in fear and fleeing inside. Salen turned with trepidation heavy in his heart; he knew what he would see. There on the horizon of the second day, as Sulan set for the evening, was a massive shadow, its wings blocking out a fair amount of light. The ground shook with its distant roar and Salen could only imagine its size if they could see it from this far away. Ravin Dar had done the impossible and called forth a dragon.

"Salen, is that what I think it is?" Shyi asked, the first words she had uttered for days. She drew her weapon reflexively and backed away as the shadow grew in size.

"Why, yes dear, it is. To answer your next question... yes it seems to be coming right for us." Salen saw the dragon then, a massive beast of scales and death. The beast was at least one hundred feet long, with a wingspan of almost two hundred feet across. Its deep red scales were almost black with Sulan's fading light behind it, yet its blazing eyes of flame shone brightly to all who beheld the creature. On its back, tiny indeed compared to the sheer enormity of the dragon, sat Ravin, his maniacal laughter echoing between the dragon's roars of superiority. The dragon had come to enact its master's revenge and they were mostly helpless to stop it.

"Salen, what are we going to do?"

"We're going to help as many of these people as we can, save ourselves, then search for a way to fight something that only existed as a story until this morning." Salen smiled despite the encroaching doom.

"How can you still smile at a time like this?"

"Because, I get to do it with a beautiful lady, of course," he said, leaning in to kiss her deeply. After all, he may never get the chance to do that again...

To be continued in:

Dragon Master

Rise of the Archmage: Book Two

Available for free, exclusively by signing up for the author's newsletter HERE[1].

Sign up today for your free book, news on release dates, cover reveals, and other exciting news!

---

1. https://tinyletter.com/Michael_D_Nadeau

About the Author

BORN IN THE USUAL WAY, author **Michael D. Nadeau** found fantasy at the age of eight with Dungeons & Dragons. He loved being different people as well as casting magic. By High school he discovered his love for reading thanks to a teacher. She fed his thirst for books by bringing her own books from home and lending them to him, even buying one towards the end of her class. He has now read hundreds of fantasy books, living in each of their worlds along with the characters. After awhile he started created his own worlds for his games with friends. Cities, gods, ancient and terrible beings and histories...then he would burn them all down.

He is the author of the Lythinall series: *The Darkness Returns* book 1, *The Darkness Within* book 2 (August 2020), *The Darkness Falls* (coming soon), and Tales from Lythinall — an anthology (coming soon). He also has several stories in Kyanite Press's Journal of speculative fiction and Eerie River

Publishing anthologies, as well as writing for Gestalt Media's monthly contest regularly.

www.ingramcontent.com/pod-product-compliance
Lightning Source LLC
Chambersburg PA
CBHW052117150726
48002CB00006B/2388